STONE ARCH **READERS**

are published by Stone Arch Books
151 Good Counsel Drive, P.O. Box 669
Mankato, Minnesota 56002
www.stonearchbooks.com

Library of Congress
Cataloging-in-Publication Data
Meister, Cari.
  Snorp, the city monster / by Cari Meister;
illustrated by Dennis Messner.
    p. cm. — (Stone Arch reader)
  ISBN 978-1-4342-1632-8 (library binding)
  ISBN 978-1-4342-1747-9 (paperback)
  [1. Tongue—Fiction.
  2. City and town life—Fiction.
  3. Monsters—Fiction.]
  I. Messner, Dennis, ill. II. Title.
  PZ7.M515916Sno 2010
  [E]—dc22   2009000887

Summary: Snorp has an
extra long tongue that
causes problems.

Creative Director: Heather Kindseth
Designer: Bob Lentz

Reading Consultants:
Gail Saunders-Smith, Ph.D.
Melinda Melton Crow, M.Ed.
Laurie K. Holland, Media Specialist

Printed in the United States of America

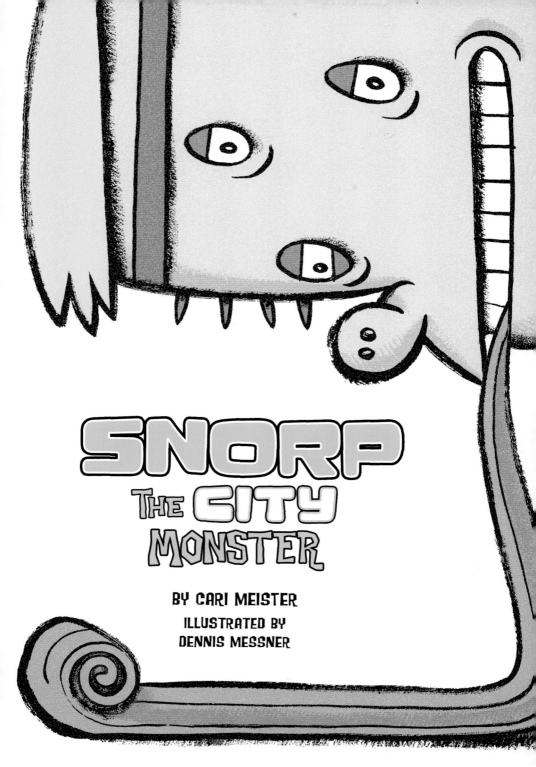

SNORP
THE CITY
MONSTER

BY CARI MEISTER

ILLUSTRATED BY
DENNIS MESSNER

STONE ARCH BOOKS
MINNEAPOLIS   SAN DIEGO

SNORP

Snorp lives in the big city.
He has a very, very long tongue.

A long tongue can be useful.
Snorp is the best window washer
in town.

It is easy for Snorp to hang
his clothes to dry.

Snorp can help his friends.

Sometimes a long tongue is
a problem. Snorp's tongue does
not fit in his mouth. It drags on
the ground.

Sometimes Snorp is in a hurry. Then his tongue is an even bigger problem.

It is very hard to talk with a long tongue. No one understands what Snorp is saying.

The baker always gives him
the wrong donuts.

The shoe monster always
gives him the wrong shoes.

One night, Snorp asks for
ham and cheese.

The waiter brings him a hat
and sheep.

Snorp went home very hungry.

"I must do something about my tongue!" Snorp says.

He tries wrapping it around his head. Now he cannot see.

He tries wearing it like a belt. Now he cannot get through the door.

"What will I do?" Snorp says.
"My tongue will always get in
the way."

The next morning, Snorp's cousin Barker comes for a visit.

"Why are you sad?" Barker asks.

Snorp tries to answer. Barker
cannot understand him.

"I know how you feel," Barker
says.

Barker opens his briefcase.
Snorp looks inside. He sees
a tongue. It is a very, very long
tongue just like his!

"Watch," says Barker. "I learned
a trick about my tongue."

Snorp's cousin takes out the tongue.

He puts it in his mouth.

Then, he pushes his nose.

Wow! Now Barker has a long
tongue too.

Barker stands on his head.
He pushes his nose again. His
tongue falls off.

He rolls it back up.

"Now you try," he says to Snorp.

Snorp stands on his head. He pushes his nose. His tongue falls off!

Snorp rolls up his tongue and puts it away. He thanks his cousin and walks to the donut shop.

Snorp tries out his short
tongue.

"I will have two chocolate
donuts and three glazed
donuts," he says. And for the
first time ever, Snorp gets the
right donuts.

Now everyone understands Snorp.

And he is still the best
window washer in town.

THE END

STORY WORDS

tongue   wrapping   chocolate

clothes   cousin   glazed

donuts   briefcase   everyone

Total Word Count: 368

MEET ALL FOUR OF OUR MONSTERS!